THE DANGERS OF DRUGS, ALCOHOL, AND SMOKING

THE DANGERS OF
TOBACCO

JENNA TOLLI

PowerKiDS
press
New York

Published in 2020 by The Rosen Publishing Group, Inc.
29 East 21st Street, New York, NY 10010

First Edition

Editor: Jenna Tolli
Book Design: Reann Nye

Photo Credits: Cover © stockstudioX/istockphoto.com; series art patpitchaya/Shutterstock.com;
p. 5 Jeff Greenberg/Universal Images Group/Getty Images; p. 6 Kittisun/Shutterstock.com;
p. 7 nnattalli/Shutterstock.com; p. 8 zairiazmal/Shutterstock.com; p. 9, 19 Bloomberg/Getty Images;
p. 11 cheapbooks/Shutterstock.com; p. 13 Elnur/Shutterstock.com; p. 14 TMA Harding/Shutterstock.com;
p. 15 Education Images/ Universal Images Group/Getty Images; p. 17 Sladic/ iStock / Getty Images
Plus/Getty Images; p. 20 Image Point Fr/Shutterstock.com; p. 21 Monkey Business Images/Shutterstock.
com; p. 22 totojang1977/Shutterstock.com.

Cataloging-in-Publication Data

Names: Tolli, Jenna.
Title: The dangers of tobacco / Jenna Tolli.
Description: New York : PowerKids Press, 2020. | Series: The dangers of drugs, alcohol, and smoking |
Includes glossary and index.
Identifiers: ISBN 9781725309906 (pbk.) | ISBN 9781725309920 (library bound) | ISBN
9781725309913 (6 pack)
Subjects: LCSH: Smoking–Juvenile literature. | Smoking–Health aspects–Juvenile literature. | Smoking–Adverse
effects–Juvenile literature. | Tobacco use–Health aspects–Juvenile literature.
Classification: LCC RC567.T65 2020 | DDC 616.86'5–dc23

Manufactured in the United States of America

Some of the images in this book illustrate individuals who are models. The depictions do not imply actual situations or events.

CPSIA Compliance Information: Batch #CWPK20. For Further Information contact Rosen Publishing, New York, New York at 1-800-237-9932.

CONTENTS

A DEADLY DRUG

Smoking cigarettes is one of the worst things someone can do to their body. Tobacco and other **chemicals** from cigarettes are what make smoking so dangerous, or unsafe, and cause lasting health problems. Tobacco use is one of the biggest public health problems in the world, and millions of people die from smoking cigarettes every year.

If tobacco causes so many problems, why do so many people keep smoking? Part of the reason is that chemicals in cigarettes are very **addictive**, which makes it hard to quit. Tobacco companies also spend billions of dollars on advertising their products.

DANGER ZONE

Every day, 1,300 people in the United States die from tobacco use—either by using the drug themselves or from being **exposed** to cigarette smoke from others.

Tobacco Facts

What About Chew and Cigars?

All kinds of tobacco are harmful.

When you use chewing tobacco or snuff, the tobacco touches the inside of your mouth, lips or nose.

When you smoke cigarettes, pipes or cigars, the chemicals in the smoke touch the inside of your mouth, nose, throat and lungs.

✗ Cigars can have up to 70 times as much nicotine as cigarettes. Even if you just hold an unlit cigar in your mouth, the chemicals get into your body.

Low-tar, low-nicotine cigarettes have less tar nicotine. But they still have chemicals to be harm

Tobacco and Other

Tobacco doesn't just harm the person who uses it. Tobacco can hurt nonsmokers, too.

✗ Nonsmokers, especially babies and young children, who breathe other people's smoke can get more colds, ear infections, allergies, lung infections and asthma.

✗ Nonsmokers can get lung disease, heart disease and cancer from being around tobacco smoke.

✗ Pregnant women who smoke pass nicotine and other chemicals to their unborn babies.

Many people around

✗ They don'
✗ They are
✗ Many other smo

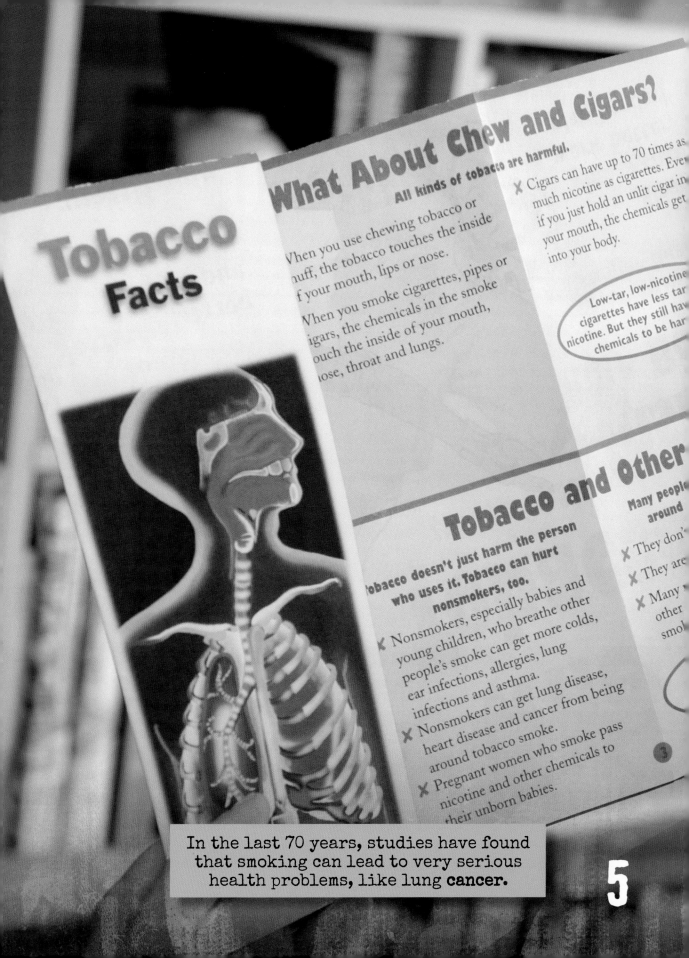

In the last 70 years, studies have found that smoking can lead to very serious health problems, like lung **cancer.**

WHAT IS TOBACCO?

Tobacco is a plant that grows in over 125 countries, including China, India, Brazil, and the United States. People have been using tobacco for thousands of years, but cigarettes started to become popular in the United States in the early and mid-1900s.

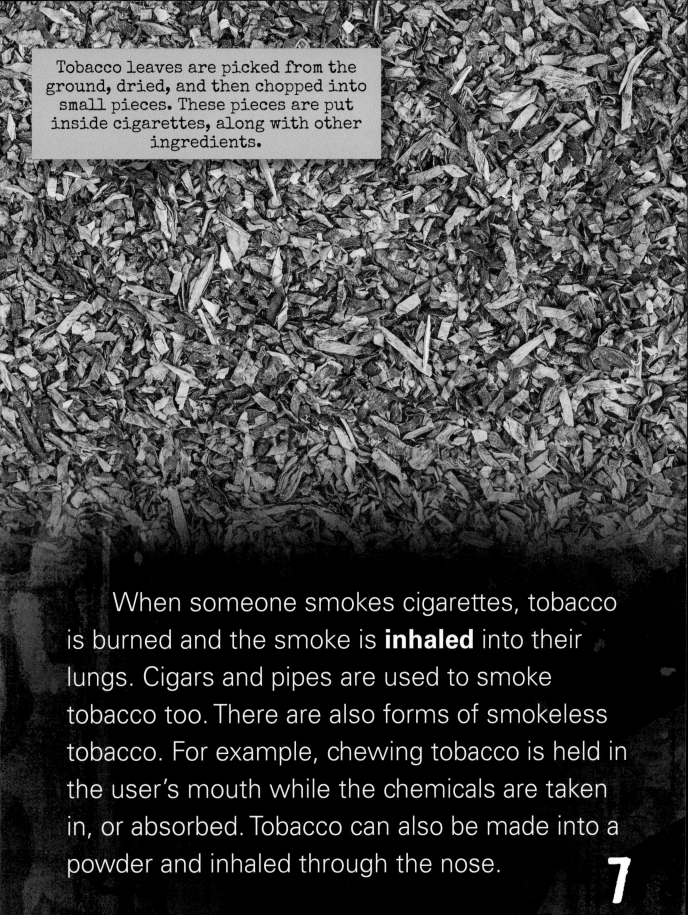

Tobacco leaves are picked from the ground, dried, and then chopped into small pieces. These pieces are put inside cigarettes, along with other ingredients.

When someone smokes cigarettes, tobacco is burned and the smoke is **inhaled** into their lungs. Cigars and pipes are used to smoke tobacco too. There are also forms of smokeless tobacco. For example, chewing tobacco is held in the user's mouth while the chemicals are taken in, or absorbed. Tobacco can also be made into a powder and inhaled through the nose.

7

HARMFUL CHEMICALS

Tobacco isn't the only dangerous **substance** in cigarettes. There are about 70 chemicals inside them that are known to cause cancer as well. Nicotine is the chemical in cigarettes that makes them so addictive. It affects certain parts of the brain that can make people feel more relaxed and improves their mood.

DANGER ZONE

Electronic cigarettes don't burn tobacco like regular cigarettes, but they are still dangerous. They have nicotine and other harmful substances that cause addiction and health problems.

In the United States, people aren't allowed to buy tobacco products until they are 18 or 21, but this still doesn't make it safe. Stores check people's ages before they sell cigarettes to anyone.

Marlboro

Smoking seriously harms you and others around you

Some of the same substances in cigarettes are also found in household items, like lead in batteries, acetone in nail polish remover, and ammonia in cleaning supplies. Tar is another product found in cigarettes, which is also used to pave roads. Tar has the most chemicals that cause cancer from cigarette smoke.

DANGERS OF ADDICTION

Nicotine is very addictive, which means smokers' brains and bodies start to depend on it. When a person quits smoking, it changes the balance of chemicals in their brain. This can lead to different problems and side effects, which are called withdrawal. Problems of withdrawl include head pain, sweating, trouble paying attention, trouble sleeping, and more. These effects can last for days or weeks.

When people stop smoking, they have **cravings** for nicotine. The cravings can be **triggered** when someone is in a place where they used to smoke or is feeling upset.

DANGER ZONE

When young people try smoking, most don't think they'll become addicted. But almost 80 percent of adult smokers started smoking before they were 18.

Everyone's experience when they quit smoking is different. Some people have worse **symptoms** than others.

11

HEALTH PROBLEMS

When someone starts smoking, some of the bad effects can be seen very quickly. They might start to cough more and lose their breath when they exercise or play sports. But many other deadly problems happen to smokers over time that you can't see.

Smoking cigarettes causes breathing problems and hurts the lungs. Smoking can lead to lung cancer. Cigarettes are also linked to many other types of cancer and are responsible for over 30 percent of cancer-related deaths. Smoking also makes it more likely that someone will have a heart attack. It hurts the immune system, which makes it harder to fight **infections**.

DANGER ZONE

Our brains continue to form until our mid-20s. When young people smoke, the chemicals from cigarettes can hurt parts of the brain that control learning, attention, and mood.

The chances of developing lung cancer are much higher for smokers than for non-smokers.

13

SECONDHAND SMOKE

When someone smokes a cigarette, the smoke they breathe out goes into the air around them. If you're near someone smoking, those harmful chemicals can get into your body as you breathe. This is called secondhand smoke.

NO VAPING
Vaping is Not Permitted
On These Premises

DANGER ZONE

Electronic cigarettes don't have the same kind of smoke as regular cigarettes, but they still let harmful chemicals into the air, like nicotine. They're banned in many public places.

NO SMOKING
NO VAPOR
NO TOBACCO USE

There are laws against smoking in many public places. Schools, parks, beaches and other places post signs outside to remind people that smoking is not allowed.

Secondhand smoke causes health problems too. Just like smoking, when people are exposed to secondhand smoke over a long period of time, it can lead to cancer, and other heart and lung problems. When children are exposed to secondhand smoke, they have a higher chance of having certain health problems, including some types of infections.

15

Sometimes it can be hard for teenagers to avoid tobacco, but simply saying "no thanks" can help.

Most kids don't smoke. The number of middle school and high school students that smoke cigarettes has gone down in recent years.

>

17

ADVERTISING

Years ago, cigarette ads used to be everywhere. But as we learned more about the dangers of smoking, the U.S. government started to make laws about how tobacco could be advertised.

Around 50 years ago, a law was passed to ban tobacco ads from TV and the radio. Warnings were also put on all cigarette packages to remind buyers that smoking is dangerous to their health. Since then, many other laws have been created to keep the public safe. For example, in 1998, tobacco companies were banned from paying film companies to advertise their brands in kids' movies.

DANGER ZONE

Tobacco companies still spend billions of dollars every year to promote their products. They advertise in stores and have sales to make products cheaper.

Over 110 countries in the world require health warnings on cigarette packages. In some countries, full-color pictures are included to show the harmful effects of smoking.

WAYS TO QUIT

Products like nicotine gum and patches have a small amount of nicotine that can help people control their cravings when they quit smoking. This is called nicotine **replacement** therapy. These products let nicotine into the body slowly, but without all of the chemicals that are in cigarettes. Over time, the amount of nicotine can be reduced, which helps people stop using them.

Every state in the U.S. has a free hotline
that smokers can call to get advice and
help when they want to quit.

It's also helpful to talk with doctors and
counselors about ways to quit smoking. When
people go to counseling for advice and support,
they have a better chance of quitting for good.
There are also support groups where smokers
can help each other quit smoking.

STAYING SAFE

Since the 1960s, the number of smokers in the United States has gone down by nearly half. In about 50 years, the rate of smoking went down from 42 percent to 18 percent. But there are still thousands of people that die from smoking every year in the United States, and millions around the world.

All forms of tobacco are dangerous. No matter how tobacco is used, there are chemicals in this drug that are proven to cause serious health problems. As we learn more about tobacco, we are finding new ways to prevent kids from starting to smoke and to help people quit smoking.

GLOSSARY

addictive: Something that causes someone to not want to stop.

cancer: A serious disease caused by cells that are not normal that can spread to parts of the body.

chemicals: Matter that can be mixed with other matter to cause changes.

craving: A strong desire for something.

exposed: Not protected or covered.

infection: A sickness caused by germs entering the body.

inhale: To breathe in.

replacement: To be used instead of something else.

substance: A material of a particular kind.

symptoms: Changes in the body or mind that show something bad.

triggered: To cause to start to happen.

INDEX

WEBSITES

Due to the changing nature of Internet links, PowerKids Press has developed an online list of websites related to the subject of this book. This site is updated regularly. Please use this link to access the list: www.powerkidslinks.com/das/tobacco